Ruth

HEY, ELEPHANT!

EY, ELEPHANT!

by Eleanor J. Lapp

illustrated by John Paul Richards

STECK-VAUGHN COMPANY • AUSTIN, TEXAS

An Intext Publisher

ISBN 0-8114-7704-5
Library of Congress Catalog Card Number 73-102099
Copyright © 1970 by Steck-Vaughn Company, Austin, Texas
All Rights Reserved
Printed and Bound in the United States of America

James found a baby elephant walking
in the alley.

"Hey, Elephant! Are you lost or something?"
The baby elephant stopped and looked at
James.

"That's right. I forgot," said James.
"Elephants don't talk. Hey, Elephant, follow
me. I'll try to find out where you belong."

"Tum-te-tum-te-tum," sang James as he turned in at his gate.

The baby elephant followed.

"Wow! How will I get you in through the doorway? Hold your breath, Elephant, and I'll push."

SLIDE!

BANG!

CRUNCH!

Elephant squeezed through the door and slid on the rug. Down went Elephant and the end table.

"Oh, no! My mother will be angry. You
had better come into my room," said James.
The baby elephant was barely small enough
to walk down the hall into James's room.

"We have peanuts for the squirrels. I'll bet you would like some of those. Here, make yourself at home," said James.

The elephant stood by the bed.

BANG! went the screen door. In came
James's mother.

"James," she said, shaking her finger, "look at this house. What a mess. Were you playing cowboy in the living room again?"

"No, Mom. I . . ."

"James, whatever the excuse is, I don't want to hear about it."

"Tum-te-tum-tum," sang James to himself.

James went into his room, and there lay
Elephant, sleeping on the floor.

James tiptoed to the bed, took the cover off,
and put it over Elephant.

Mom went by the door.

"James, straighten your bed. It looks like a pile of lumps and bumps."

"Mom, I . . ."

"No excuses. You're big enough to make your bed."

"Tum-te-tum-tum," sang James softly. He didn't want to wake Elephant.

SNORE!

SNORE!

SNOOOOORE!

Elephant was really sleeping.

"What is that strange noise?" James's mother called as she was making dinner. "Are you catching a cold, James?"

James came out of his room and closed the door gently.

"Tum-te-tum-tum. I feel fine, Mom, but . . ."

"James, run to the corner store and get some milk," said Mother.

While James was gone, his mother heard a
strange clumping sound in the house. "That
boy is up to something," she said to herself.
She tiptoed down the hall and opened the
bedroom door. It would only open a crack. It
would just not open any more. The bedcover
lay in a heap on the floor.

"Tum-te-tum-tum," James sang as he walked into the house.

"James, you haven't cleaned up your room. It's such a mess that the door won't open. The bedcover is on the floor. March right in there and clean it up."

"Mom, I . . ."

"Right now, James!"

Elephant backed away from the door as James came into the bedroom. He watched as James put the cover back on the bed. He watched as James picked up the toys.

Then SLUUUP! Elephant drank most of the water in the goldfish bowl. The fish hid under a seashell.

"Oh! Now you're thirsty," James said.

James went into the kitchen for a pan of water.

"James, what are you doing now?" asked Mother.

"Water for my elephant," said James.

"Now, James, stop teasing," said Mother.

"Tum-te-tum-tum," sang James as he walked away with the water.

"SLUUUP!" went Elephant, drinking the pan of water.

James made four more trips for water.

"That's enough," said Mother. "You're just playing with that water."

Father came home. James tried to tell him about Elephant.

"Not now. I want to read the paper. Tell me your story after dinner," said Father.

James finished his dinner.

"Time for your bath, James," said Mother.

"Tum-te-tum-tum. Could I play with something in the bathtub?"

"Yes, but no water on the floor." Mother started the bath water.

"Shh," said James, as Elephant clumped
behind him into the bathroom.

GURGLE!

SPLASH!

SWISH!

Elephant and James took a bath.

"James, be careful in that bathtub," called Mother from the kitchen.

Elephant sprayed James and blew supersize soap bubbles. James used five towels to dry Elephant.

Then James put on his pajamas and went to say good-night.

"Hey—Dad?" James tugged on his father's sleeve.

Dad had fallen asleep after dinner.

"Dad?"

"You had better talk to him in the morning, James," said Mother.

"Good-night, Mom. Tum-te-tum-tum."

James covered Elephant with the bedcover.
Then he closed the door so the snores
wouldn't wake Mom and Dad.

The next morning James was up early.
Elephant was gone! While Mom and Dad were
still sleeping, James tiptoed out to the living
room, looked in the garden, then walked
out to the alley.

A man with a red cap and coat was leading
Elephant down the alley.

"Hey, mister!" called James.

"Hi, boy. I just found the elephant that
walked away from the circus train yesterday.
He looks in good shape."

Elephant looked at James, then seemed to wave good-by with his trunk.

"Good-by, Elephant," said James softly.

"Tum-te-tum-tum," sang James as he went
back into the house.

Mom was in the kitchen making coffee.

"James, were you outside in your pajamas?
Put on your clothes."

"Yes, Mom. Tum-te-tum-tum," sang James
as he walked down the hall.